Who cares about
law and order?

illustrated by **Pam Adams**

Published by Child's Play (International) Ltd

© M. Twinn 1991   ISBN 0-85953-364-6 (hard cover)   Printed in Singapore
ISBN 0-85953-354-9 (soft cover)

Babies are helpless.
They depend on their parents
to look after them.

From the day we are born,
we cannot have everything we want.
We cannot be everything we would like to be,
or do everything we want to do.

Because people live together
and depend on one another,
there have to be rules.

When we are children,
our parents make the rules.

But they don't always explain them.

Why should we keep clean?

Why do I have to be tidy?

Why should we be polite and helpful?

Why shouldn't we eat junk food?
Why shouldn't we play in dangerous places?

Why should we be home before dark?
Why shouldn't we talk to strangers?

Parents are not always easy to understand.
But they make rules for our own good.

They often do what we want, instead of what they want.

When we have friends,
we learn that sharing is fun!
Playing is more important than winning.
We have to keep to the rules.

Sometimes, we lose our temper,
say bad things, or want to fight.

In the end, we swallow our pride,
say "Sorry!" and are friends again.

Without friends, life is lonely.
Everybody needs friends.

In sport, we try hard to win.
Wanting to win makes us think we are right.
So there have to be referees or umpires.
We have to accept what they say.

In school, there are rules, too.
If we want to learn, we have to behave.

We have to be punctual, pay attention,
do as we are told and keep quiet.

Teachers are patient. They understand.
They have a sense of humour.

If they didn't, they couldn't teach.

Sometimes, it is fun to break the rules.
As long as nobody is hurt or upset.

Bullies and gangs make their own rules.
They make life miserable for the rest of us.

The older we are,
the more we learn to treat others
the way we want them to treat us.

Living together is impossible,
if we all do what we want.

When we grow up, rules are just as important!

We have to earn a living.
Rules help us to work better and keep us safe.

We have to obey the laws of our country, too.

They are made by our government.

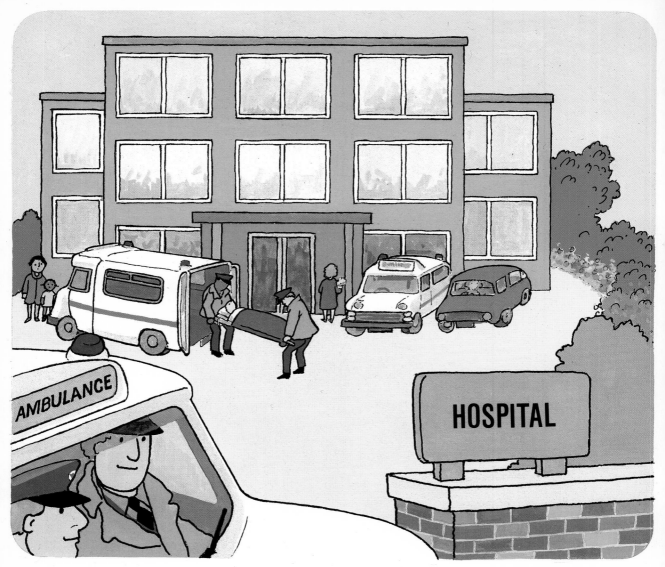

Some laws ensure that our nation is run properly.

We have to pay taxes for roads, hospitals, schools and police.

Some laws are good manners,
like not making a noise when people are sleeping.

Some laws protect us from those
who want to hurt us,
or rob us, or cheat us.

The police help to make sure
that laws are obeyed.
They try to be fair and don't take sides.

The police need our help. They cannot be everywhere.

We can watch out for our neighbours
and report anything suspicious.

If we break the law, we may be tried in court.
A judge makes sure we have a fair trial.
A jury of people like ourselves may decide
whether we are telling the truth. It is not easy.

We may go to court to settle a disagreement.
We will have to pay lawyers to argue our case.
It is better than taking the law into our own hands.

Win or lose, we must accept the court's decision.

As long as people are selfish, greedy, envious,
bad-tempered, violent and untruthful,
as long as we disagree and argue,
we will need laws, police, judges and lawyers.

We will never agree about everything.
Laws will never be perfect.
Life will never be fair.

But we can learn to care for one another,
respect each other's ideas,
and defend each other's rights.